SEBASTIAN

IS ALWAYS LATE

Written by Anne-Marie Chapouton

Illustrated by Chantal van den Berghe

North-South Books

On Friday Miss Jessy said,
"Why Sebastian, this is the first day this week
you haven't been late.
What happened?"

"On Monday I hitched a ride
on a shooting star

and a flying carpet.

On Tuesday I came in an enormous balloon.
It had flowers painted all over it.

I crossed the pond
on a flying fish.
That was really great!

Wednesday was fun, too, when I flew
on the soft feathery back
of a big white goose.

Then I caught the tail
of a kite

and arrived at school
on a hang glider.

But that was a bit scary.
So on Thursday I came in a
real airplane.
The pilot lowered a long rope
to pick me up at home

and I parachuted down
when we were over the school.

But today, Miss Jessy...

...I just walked."